I0727940

Nobody's Nino

Freshwater Horizon Press

Texas

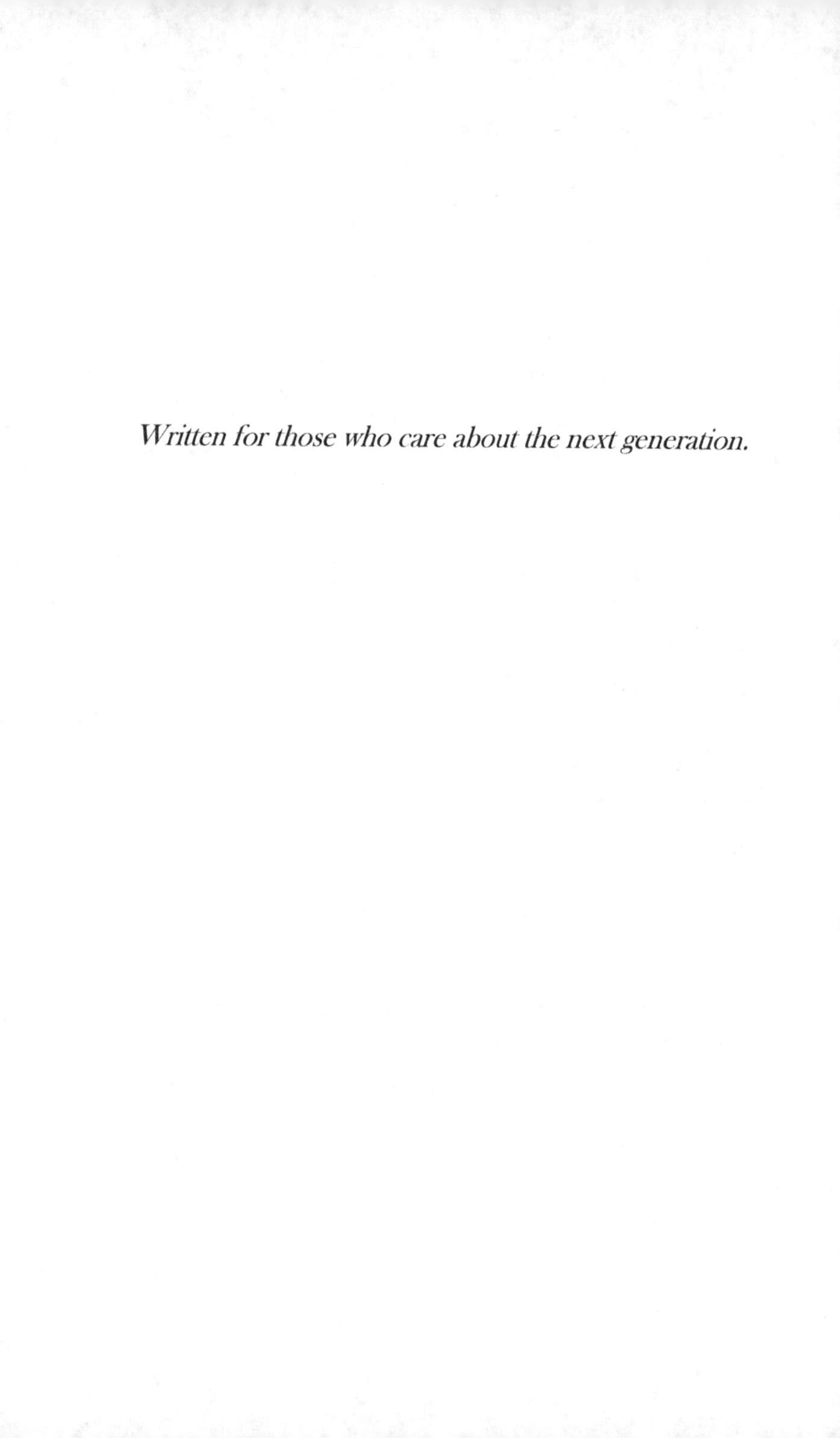

Written for those who care about the next generation.

Chapter 1
Nino Robert

When I was a chamaco, maybe eight or nine, I thought my Nino Roberto was the strongest man in the world.

Not the President.

Not the Pope.

Not even the luchadores on Channel 26 with their shiny masks and big panza muscles.

No — my nino was bigger than all of them.

He had these rough hands, always smelling like gasoline and limón cleaner, the kind of hands that could fix a car, build a fence, and swat you upside the head — all before breakfast. But when he put one of those hands on my shoulder, gently, like he was choosing to be soft… I felt like the whole world could fall apart and we'd still be okay.

"Mijo, people think strength is in the fists," he'd say while tightening a bolt or polishing a wrench. "Pero la fuerza de verdad… it's in the corazón. You hear me?"

I always nodded, even when I didn't understand.

That was the thing about him — you wanted to understand.

You wanted to grow into his words.

Every Sunday he'd pick me up in his old white Chevy C10, the one with the cracked dashboard and the Virgen de Guadalupe sticker fading on the rear window. We'd go for pan dulce at Bowie Bakery, and he'd let me choose one thing, no más uno, because "a man learns control through his stomach."

I always picked the same thing — a marranito.

He always pretended to be surprised.

He'd laugh, that deep chest laugh, warm enough to turn winter into spring.

"Ay, Emilio… you're predictable, mijo. One day you gotta surprise the world."

Back then, I believed everything he said was a prophecy.

I believed I'd be someone someday — not famous, not rich — just someone. Someone good. Someone solid. Someone like him.

And then… he died.

Just like that.

One heart attack on a Tuesday morning.

One minute he was teaching me how to sand down a piece of wood without leaving uneven grooves, and the next minute my mom was crying in the kitchen, telling

me to sit down, por favor mijo, siéntate, like the chair
was going to save me.

But nothing saved me that day.

Not the chair.

Not the rosary hanging on the wall.

Not even the stories he left behind.

I didn't cry at the funeral.

I stared at his casket like I expected him to get up and say
something wise about how death was just another job to
finish.

But he didn't get up.

And after everyone left, I stayed behind, standing there in
my little white shirt with the crooked collar.

I put my hand on the casket — the way he used to put his hand on my shoulder — and whispered:

"I'm gonna be a nino like you. One day. I promise."

I didn't know then how rare it was. How in our culture, somebody has to choose you. How even good men, great men, might never get asked. How being a nino wasn't just about showing up to a baptism — it was a title, a responsibility, a bond deeper than blood.

I didn't know any of that.

I just knew I wanted to be like him.

Wanted to give the kind of strength he gave me.

Wanted to be wanted the way he made me feel wanted.

I held onto that promise for years. Carried it in the same pocket where I kept my shop rags and loose screws. A quiet little hope I never told anyone about.

Because some dreams, you keep close.

Some dreams are too tender for the world.

And for a long time — longer than I'd ever admit —

I believed I'd be nobody's nino.

But life…

Life has its own way of surprising you.

Even when you think your story already ended.

Even when you think the world forgot you.

Even when you think you're just a mechanic in an old shop with grease under his nails and a dream that never came true.

Because all it takes is one kid —

one broken, scared, overlooked kid —

walking through your door…

…to change everything.

Chapter 2

A Lifetime of Almosts

Life moves fast when you're not paying attention.

One minute you're a skinny kid in church shoes too tight for your toes, and the next you're a grown man squinting under the hood of a car, telling some younger mechanic, "Careful with that bolt, cabron, that thing strips easy."

That's how it happens.

You don't notice the years.

They just sneak up behind you and say, Surprise, viejo. You're old now.

I didn't become a famous man.

I became something better.

I became trusted.

By twenty-five I had my first garage job. By thirty-five I had my own shop. By forty I had calluses thicker than most men's pride and a reputation that followed me like a proper shadow.

People would ask,

"Where should I take my truck?"

And somebody else would answer,

"Vargas. Siempre Vargas."

That felt good.

But when your dreams are small and quiet, nobody claps for them.

They just live inside you like a soft ache.

I married young. Had kids quick. Life didn't give us time to think — just to do. And we did everything. Homework. Bills. Soccer practice. Doctor appointments. Worrying.

And my kids?

They did better than anyone expected.

Air Force, all three of 'em.

First one became a teacher.

Second went into medicine.

Third law school.

I used to sit in church and look at them from the pew like they were borrowed angels.

I'd thank God quietly.

Gracias, Señor… even if you never give me nothing else.

But Sundays are funny like that.

They make you count both blessings and losses.

I'd sit through baptisms and weddings and confirmations and see other men step forward — godfathers with their pressed shirts, polished shoes, and proud eyes.

Every time the priest would ask:

"Who stands as padrino?"

Every time, my chest would tighten.

Not jealousy.

Something worse.

Absence.

Like a seat at a table that never had my name on it.

People assumed I had godchildren.

They'd ask it like they were asking what kind of dog I owned.

"You got any ahijados?"

And I'd smile.

"Not yet."

Years passed.

Still nothing.

Now don't get me wrong — I had respect.
Friends. A good wife. Beautiful kids. A roof. A
shop that kept food on the table and grease on
my hands.

But some dreams don't age well.

Some dreams just sit there waiting.

Every year I got older, the little boy inside me
got quieter.

Eventually, he stopped asking.

I didn't talk about Nino Roberto anymore.

Didn't talk about promises or dreams or anything
that made your voice crack.

A man learns to swallow certain things.

So I swallowed that.

Told myself:

Maybe being a nino isn't for everybody.

Maybe it was just a kid's dream.

Maybe it already passed me by.

But every now and then, late at night, when the shop was quiet and the tools were put away, I'd sit on a milk crate behind my office, the same place where the radio barely came in clear…

…and I'd think of his voice.

La fuerza de verdad… it's in the corazón.

I'd touch my chest — not dramatic, not crying
— just checking.

Still there.

Still hurting a little.

Still hoping more than I wanted to admit.

And then one afternoon —

on a day just like any other —

life decided to knock on my shop door real loud.

Not with a miracle.

Not with music.

But with a man who smelled like beer and
disappointment…

16

…

and a boy who didn't even know he was about to
be chosen.

Chapter 3
The Shop

My shop wasn't fancy.

No neon lights.

No glass doors.

No waiting room with free cafecito and a TV stuck on Telemundo.

Just concrete floors stained by a thousand oil changes and walls painted the color of tired dreams. But it was mine. Every crack, every bolt, every crooked shelf — built with my hands or paid for with my sweat.

Vargas Auto & Body.

The sign out front leaned a little to the left, like it had given up on standing straight a long time ago. I kept meaning to fix it, same way I kept meaning to fix a lot of things.

But customers found me anyway.

Mornings smelled like gasoline and fresh tortillas from the panadería next door. Radios fought each other all day — Vicente Fernández in one corner, classic rock in the other — both losing to the sound of engines coughing back to life.

I liked it that way.

Noise keeps you honest.

By noon, my shirt usually looked like I'd been in a fistfight with a car and lost. My hands stayed black no matter how much Fast Orange I used. Some things don't wash off.

I had a couple of muchachos working for me — good kids, worked hard, complained too much. They were always asking questions.

"Hey, boss, is this bolt supposed to wiggle?"

"No, mijo. Nothing should wiggle in a man's life."

They'd laugh, even if they didn't know what I meant.

Customers waited on old folding chairs by the soda machine that ate their quarters. Some of them came in angry. Most left smiling.

That's what happens when someone fixes the thing you depend on.

Cars bring out people's real personalities.

You learn quick who panics, who prays, and who lies.

Around two-thirty every afternoon, when the sun was mean and the asphalt looked like it could melt a man through his boots, I'd step into my office and open my old lunchbox.

Same thing every day:

Beans.

Rice.

Two tortillas.

Simple food makes a simple man.

That day was no different.

I took my first bite…

…when the bell above the door rang.

Not the delicate kind of ring.

More like a BOING, like the thing was tired of being used.

I wiped my hands and came out from behind the counter.

That's when I saw them.

The father walked in first.

Chest out.

Belly before everything.

Looked like a man who fought life and lost but still wanted a rematch.

The boy followed — skinny, shoulders curved inward like he was carrying something too heavy for his age.

He didn't make eye contact.

Kept his eyes on the floor like it might save him.

The man didn't waste time.

"Hey, you hiring?"

No hello.

No respect.

Just need.

I wiped my hands on my rag.

"Depends," I said. "Who's asking?"

The man jerked a thumb backward.

"This one."

The kid flinched.

"He's gotta do something," the man continued, loud like the boy couldn't hear. "Can't learn. Bad in school. Gets into fights but can't even fight right. Teachers always calling. I'm tired of dealing with him."

The boy's ears went red.

I felt something shift inside my chest — slow, deep, dangerous.

The father kept going:

"Figured maybe he can sweep floors or something. He ain't good for much else. Kid's a nobody."

The shop went quiet.

Even the radio seemed to lower its voice.

I stared at the man — really stared.

Then I said:

"Let me ask you something."

The man crossed his arms.

"Sure."

"You think a garage is a place for nobodies?"

He blinked.

"Well, no, I—"

"Because every car in here belongs to someone who counts on it. Someone who loves it. Someone who trusts it to get their kids to school and their wife to work."

He shifted his weight.

"I didn't mean—"

"And you think the men who fix those cars are nobodies too?"

Now he looked nervous.

"I was just trying to say the kid—"

I raised my hand.

"No."

Silence.

I looked at the boy.

Still staring at the floor.

Then I looked back at the father.

"I'll take him."

The man exhaled like he'd just won something.

"But one condition."

The man nodded eagerly.

"Anything."

I leaned forward — not angry, not loud — just… serious.

"You don't question my ways."

The man hesitated.

Then smiled.

"Deal."

And just like that…

A man who thought the boy was a nobody walked into my shop.

And a boy who thought he was nothing walked into the beginning of his life.

CHAPTER 4

The Nobody

The father left fast.

Not even five minutes of pretending he cared.

No handshake.
No instructions.
Didn't even look back.

Just pointed at the boy one last time and said:

"Don't embarrass me."

Then he walked out like he'd dropped off broken equipment.

The door swung shut behind him.

The bell rattled.

And suddenly the shop felt ten times bigger.

The boy stood there frozen, skinny arms pressed tight against his sides like they were the only thing holding him together.

I watched him for a second.

Not with pity.

With memory.

Because I recognized that look.

That wasn't fear.

That was waiting for the next hit.

"Come here," I told him.

Not soft. Not mean.

Just real.

He walked over slow, like he was stepping onto ice.

"What's your name, mijo?"

His voice was so quiet I almost missed it.

"Tomás."

Not Tommy.

Not yet.

"Tomás," I repeated, letting it sit on my tongue right. "Good name."

That surprised him.

Good names surprise boys who grow up feeling unwanted.

"Have you ever held a wrench?"

He shook his head.

I reached into my toolbox and handed him a small one.

He gripped it tight like it might bite.

"That's not a snake," I said.

The boy blinked.

I smiled a little.

"Relax."

I showed him how to hold it.

Where to put his thumb.

Where to place his weight.

Then I walked him over to a busted old tire I kept leaning against the wall.

"First lesson," I said.
"You don't rush a job.

You don't curse a job.
And you never pretend you did it when you didn't."

I knelt down and loosened a bolt.

"Ahora tú."

He tried.

Failed.

Tried again.

His cheeks turned red.

His hands shook.

"Take your time."

He exhaled slowly like I'd taught him something without realizing it.

Then...

Crack.

The bolt loosened.

His eyes widened.

He looked at me like he'd just performed a trick.

I nodded.

"Again."

He did it.

Another bolt.

Another.

Then he stopped and stared at the tire like it was magic.

"Good," I said.
"Really good."

He looked at me like he thought I was lying.

I wasn't.

An hour later, his hands were dirty.
His posture looked different.
His face looked… lighter.

Not happy.

Just not crushed.

I gave him a broom.

"Tómatelo en serio," I told him.
"Don't sweep like a kid. Sweep like a man."

He nodded serious like I'd just handed him a weapon.

And then…

It happened.

A customer walked in while the boy was sweeping.

A big guy with a loud voice and impatience in his walk.

The boy froze.

Dropped the broom.

His shoulders collapsed like something inside him snapped.

I watched his chest rise fast.

Panic.

Familiar.

I stepped in.

"Tomás," I said.

Not loud.
Not angry.

Just sure.

He looked up.

"Pick it up."

He hesitated.

I waited.

His hands trembled — but he grabbed the broom.

"Finish your line."

He obeyed.

One straight line.

Then another.

The man watched.
Confused.

I stared him down.

"He's working," I said.
"We don't rush work here."

The customer nodded, quieting down like a kid caught misbehaving.

Tomás finished.

Slow.

Precise.

When he was done, he looked at me.

I nodded.

He walked away without dropping his eyes this time.

After he disappeared into the back, I leaned against the counter.

It hit me then.

Not like lightning.

Like realization.

That boy wasn't broken.

He was empty.

And nobody had ever tried to fill him with anything good.

So I decided something right there.

Quietly.

Firm.

That boy would not leave my shop the same way he came in.

Not if I had anything to say about it.

And I did.

CHAPTER 5

The Agreement

Tomás came back the next day.

That's when I knew something mattered.

Kids like him don't return to places where they feel
small.
They disappear.
Fall through cracks.

But there he was at 7:12 a.m. — seventeen minutes early
— standing outside my shop with a backpack hanging
too low on his shoulders like it was full of rocks.

I unlocked the door and he straightened up like a soldier.

"Morning," he said, nervous but trying.

"You're early."

He nodded fast.
Didn't know if that was good or bad.

I unlocked the door.

"Good," I said.

That's all it took.

We didn't talk much that day.

I showed him how to organize tools.
How to clean parts.
How to hand me things before I asked.

He watched everything.

Not like a bored kid.

Like a starving one.

I caught him copying how I stood.
How I wiped my hands.
How I talked to customers.

Not mocking.

Learning.

At lunch we sat on the milk crates in the back.

I opened my lunchbox.

He watched me like I was about to perform surgery.

I broke a tortilla in half and handed it to him.

"Eat."

He hesitated.

Kids learn hunger differently.

Some from empty kitchens.

Some from empty hearts.

"Go ahead," I said.

He did.

Then…

He smiled.

Not big.

Not loud.

Just enough to remind me he was still a kid.

That afternoon, Ray showed up.

Unannounced.

Not scheduled.

Just stormed in like he owned air.

"Hey," he yelled. "How's he doing?"

Tomás froze.

The way a deer knows when the hunter walks by.

Ray walked toward him.

"You mess anything up yet?"

Tomás opened his mouth.

Nothing came out.

I stepped forward.

"Don't do that."

Ray laughed.

"Do what?"

"Talk to him like that in front of me."

Ray's grin faded.

"He's my kid."

I nodded.

"But he works for me when he's here."

Ray crossed his arms.

"Look, I just wanted to make sure he wasn't causing you trouble. He's not exactly—"

"Finished," I said.

Ray looked confused.

"Finished what?"

"That sentence."

Silence.

Ray huffed.

"You're getting soft on him already."

I leaned closer.

Not aggressive.

Just enough to be heard.

"You brought him to me. I told you the condition."

Ray swallowed.

"Yeah, I know…"

"Then respect it."

Tomás stood behind me.

Still.

Quiet.

Watching.

Ray raised his hands.

"Alright, alright. I'm just saying—"

I cut him off gently… but firmly.

"You don't build men by tearing them down."

Ray stared like he'd never heard that before.

Maybe he hadn't.

"That boy is here to learn something," I continued.
"If you want to help him — good.
If you don't — stay out of the way."

Ray looked at Tomás.

Then back at me.

Then down at the floor.

"Fine," he muttered.

And just like that, the feud ended.

Not loudly.

Not violently.

Just settled like dust.

After Ray left, I turned to Tomás.

"You okay?"

He nodded too fast.

I crouched down so we were eye-level.

"Listen to me, mijo…
Nothing that man says in this shop is law."

He looked confused.

"In here," I told him, tapping his chest,
"You're not a nobody."

He didn't say anything.

But something unlocked behind his eyes.

Something small.

Something powerful.

That night, after the shop closed, I stayed sitting on my milk crate.

Thinking.

I hadn't meant to start something.

I just meant to save a kid from drowning.

But sometimes…

You don't realize you jumped into deep water…

…until you're already swimming.

CHAPTER 6

The First Lesson

Tomás showed up the next morning with cleaned shoes.

Not new.
Not fancy.

Just… clean.

That told me something.

Kids clean shoes when they're trying not to disappoint.

He stood by the door as I unlocked the shop like he
didn't want to step on the floor until I said it was okay.

"You scared of ghosts or what?" I asked.

He smiled shyly.

"No, sir."

"Then come in."

He did.

I didn't hand him a broom that day.

I handed him a screwdriver.

And that's how I knew it was serious.

We worked on a blue Toyota with a busted headlight.

Simple job.

But simple doesn't mean small.

I popped the hood open.

"Look," I said.

Not loud.

Not fast.

Just clear.

I explained bulbs and sockets and wiring until his eyes widened like he'd cracked open a secret.

I let him do every step.

Every one.

He dropped the bulb once.

Flinched.

I waited.

Nothing happened.

No yelling.

No insults.

Just patience.

"Pick it up," I said.

His hands shook a little.

Then steadied.

When the headlight came on, he jumped back like it bit him.

Then he laughed.

Not loud.

Not wild.

But real.

First real laugh I'd heard from him.

"What did you learn?" I asked.

He thought.

Then said:

"That it works… if you don't give up."

I smiled.

"Good."

He didn't know it yet…

But he just passed his first test.

Later, I sat him down at my desk.

The dusty one with the crooked drawer that never closed right.

I slid a piece of paper toward him.

"What's this?" he asked.

"A list," I said.

"Of what?"

"Rules."

He leaned forward.

Serious again.

The Rules (written in ink, on yellow paper):

1. **You show up early. Nobody trusts late.**
2. **You listen twice before you speak once.**
3. **You don't lie, even if it costs you.**
4. **You don't steal — time, tools, or trust.**
5. **You work with pride or we don't work at all.**
6. **You treat women like treasure, not trophies.**
7. **You never hit first… but you finish what you start.**
8. **You don't quit on bad days.**
9. **You say thank you. Even when you're mad.**
10. **You never say you're a nobody. Not here. Not ever.**

He read it slow.

Like it mattered.

He pointed at Rule Ten.

"What if I mess up?"

I leaned forward.

"Then you clean it up."

He looked at me.

"For how long?"

"As long as you're here."

Then I signed it.

Emilio Vargas

I slid the pen to him.

"You sign too."

He hesitated.

Then did.

His handwriting looked… young.

But it was his.

Something about that mattered.

When he left that day, he didn't rush out.

He stood by the door a second.

Like he wanted to say something.

Didn't.

I didn't push him.

Some kids talk when they're ready.

But as he closed the shop door behind him…

I caught myself whispering something I hadn't said out loud in years.

"Gracias, Nino Roberto."

Because somehow…

Without even knowing how…

I had just started being someone I promised I would.

CHAPTER 7

Hands and Heart

Tomás didn't just work at the shop.

The shop started living inside him.

He learned quick that grease didn't come out easy, no matter how hard you scrubbed. Some stains were earned. Some stayed for life. He started coming in with bandaids on his knuckles like badges of honor… like a mechanic's Purple Heart medal. These injuries were not from fighting — they were from learning.

And learning always draws blood.

I worked him hard.

Not cruel.

Purposeful.

There's a difference.

He'd sweep until straight lines covered the floor like art. Then I made him erase it — mop it up — and do it again.

"Why?" he once asked.

I looked at him.

"So you learn that good work isn't about being seen."

Another day, I handed him a carburetor and sent him to the back.

"Clean it."

He came back an hour later thinking he was done.

I handed it back.

"Do it again."

He sighed — too loud.

I waited.

He looked at me.

Then down at the carburetor.

Didn't argue.

Went back.

That's how you tell the difference between boys and men.

Men go back.

The hardest days were never mechanical.

They were emotional.

Some afternoons, he'd grow quiet. Short answers.
Shoulders hunched.

Those were the days I sat beside him without talking.

Silence teaches better than speeches.

One day he finally broke.

"I'm stupid," he muttered while scrubbing parts.

I didn't answer.

He tried again.

"I really am."

I stopped my wrench.

The shop stopped breathing.

"Say it again," I said.

He did.

"I'm stupid."

I walked over and set my hand on the engine between us.

"You know why this thing runs?" I asked.

He shrugged.

"Because each part does what it's supposed to."

I nodded.

"Same with people."

He didn't understand yet.

So I kept going.

"You're not stupid. You're underbuilt. That's all. You never got the right tools."

He stared.

"Tools?"

"Patience. Discipline. Confidence. Someone to tell you you're not trash."

His eyes burned.

"Who told you that?"

"My dad."

I exhaled slow through my nose.

"Then your dad is wrong."

The words landed heavy.

But true words always do.

Later that week, a customer tried to cheat us. Claimed we broke something we didn't.

Tomás watched me handle it.

Calm.

Firm.

No yelling.

No folding.

I didn't pay the man to go away.

I didn't insult him.

I stood my ground.

The customer eventually folded instead.

Afterwards, Tomás asked:

"Aren't you scared people will leave?"

I wiped my hands.

"They just leave your shop…"

I tapped his chest.

"…or they leave you empty."

He nodded.

Some lessons don't need notebooks.

Others came slower.

Talking to women.

Looking people in the eye.

Holding doors open.

Saying thank you.

Saying sorry.

Saying please.

Small things.

But small things build big men.

One afternoon after close, I handed him a hammer.

Not for work.

For the wood.

"Come."

We walked behind the shop where a broken shed leaned like it was tired of standing.

I pointed.

"Build something."

"From what?"

I kicked a pile of scrap wood.

"From mistakes."

He started wrong.

Measured wrong.

Nailed wrong.

I didn't stop him.

Eventually he stepped back.

"It's ugly."

"So is most growth."

By sunset, it stood.

Leaning.

But standing.

He ran his fingers across the wood.

Made it real.

I saw something in his face then.

Not pride.

Belief.

That night, he walked home differently.

Back straight.

Eyes forward.

Like he finally knew where his feet were.

And that's when I understood something dangerous…

I wasn't just teaching him skills.

I was teaching him who he was about to become.

CHAPTER 8

The Gym

The first time I took Tomás to the gym, he thought I was joking.

We drove past the nicer places — the ones with glass windows, new equipment, music too loud, and people pretending to sweat — and pulled up to a little old-school boxing gym tucked behind a tire shop.

The sign said **"El Mundo Boxing Club"**, but half the letters didn't light up anymore, so it mostly looked like **"El Bo ng Club."**

The place smelled like leather, sweat, VapoRub, and pride — real pride, the kind earned from bleeding a little on purpose.

Tomás hesitated at the door.

"You… you want me to fight?"

I shook my head.

"No. I want you to learn."

"Learn what?"

I pushed the door open.

"Your feet."

Inside, the old wooden floor creaked like it was telling old stories. Heavy bags dangled from chains like sleeping giants. Posters of legends — Chávez, Salvador Sánchez, Morales — were peeling off the walls.

The kind of place where boys come in silent and leave believing.

Coach Manny looked up from wrapping a kid's hands.

"Emilio," he said, "you finally brought me a protégé or what?"

I shrugged.

"Depends if he listens."

Tomás blinked.

"I listen."

Coach Manny smirked.

"We'll see."

I didn't put gloves on him that first day.

I didn't let him punch anything.

I made him stand in front of the mirror.

"Hands up," I said.

He did.

Too high.

"Relax your shoulders."

He did.

Too much.

"Feet apart."

He did.

Too wide.

I stepped behind him and adjusted him like you adjust a crooked picture frame.

"There," I said. "That's balance."

He stared at himself.

Like he didn't recognize the stance.

Then it hit me:

He wasn't used to seeing himself *prepared* for anything.

Manny put him on footwork drills.

In boxing, I learned that footwork is crucial. It is the foundation for power, defense, ring control, and like a car engine… FORCE. Now it was time to teach Tomás.

Forward. Backward. Side to side.

He stumbled at first.

Fell once.

Turned red.

Waited for anger.

Nobody yelled.

Nobody called him dumb.

Nobody told him he was a nobody.

Manny just clapped his hands.

"Again, mijo."

And Tomás did.

Over and over.

Until his shirt stuck to his back.

Until his breath came heavy.

Until he didn't look scared anymore — just determined.

After an hour, he leaned on the ropes, exhausted.

I tossed him a water bottle.

"Why am I doing this?" he asked between gulps.

"To learn control," I said.

"Of fighting?"

"No."

I tapped his forehead with one finger.

"Of this."

He looked at me like he wanted to argue — but couldn't.

Because deep down he knew:

His fists weren't his problem.

His fear was.

Before we left, Manny stopped him.

"You ever been in a real fight?"

Tomás lowered his eyes.

"Yeah."

"Win any?"

He shook his head.

Manny lifted his chin gently — the way men who know
pain soften their hands with kids who know it too.

"You don't lose fights because you're weak," Manny
said.
"You lose because you don't think you're allowed to win
yet."

Tomás swallowed hard.

Something shifted behind his eyes.

Again.

That week became routine.

Shop.
Gym.
Walk home.

Slowly…
His steps got lighter.
His shoulders wider.
His voice steadier.

He wasn't ready to fight anyone.

But he was finally learning how not to fight himself.

And that — I knew — was the beginning of something dangerous…

Because once a boy stops punching his own shadow…

He starts becoming a man.

CHAPTER 9

School

If the shop taught Tomás how to use his hands…
and the gym taught him how to use his feet…

…school was supposed to teach him how to use
everything else.

But classrooms can be cruel in ways fists never are.

He told me once — quietly, like he was confessing a sin
— that school felt like trying to read a map in the dark.
Everyone else knew where they were going. He just
pretended he did.

And pretending takes energy.

More energy than learning.

One Tuesday afternoon, he walked into the shop
dragging his backpack like it was full of cement.

He didn't say hi.

Didn't smile.

Just went straight to the back and started sweeping, too fast, too angry.

I watched him from my workbench.

He only swept like that when he was trying not to break.

After a few minutes, he dropped the broom.

Not on purpose.

Like his hand just gave up.

I walked over.

"School?"

He nodded once.

I waited.

Kids talk in pieces — like they're handing you broken glass.

"She said… I'm not trying," he muttered.

"Who?"

"My teacher."

"What happened?"

"I got a 58 on my quiz."

I sat on the milk crate.

He stayed standing, like he didn't deserve to sit until he earned it.

"What did you study?"

"All of it."

"How long?"

"Like an hour."

I raised an eyebrow.

"Mijo… you don't get strong in the gym in one hour. Why would your brain be different?"

He didn't answer.

He just looked… tired.

Not sleepy tired.

Soul tired.

The kind of tired kids shouldn't know yet.

So I grabbed a wrench and pointed to the blue Toyota from the week before.

"You fixed that headlight," I said.

He blinked.

"Yeah… but what does that have to do—?"

"You fixed it because I broke it down into steps. One at a time. Not all at once."

He frowned.

"School is the same thing, Tomás.
You're trying to lift the whole car instead of one bolt."

He looked at the ground.

"I just… I don't want to be dumb."

I exhaled slow.

Dumb.

That word.

That poison.

Someone had fed him that word like medicine.

"You're not dumb," I said.
"You're untrained."

He looked up.

Slow.

Hopeful.

Maybe.

"Bring me your homework."

He froze.

"Right now?"

"Sí."

He ran outside, came back with his backpack, and
dumped everything on my workbench like an offering.

Math worksheets.
Vocabulary pages.
A crumpled quiz with a red 58 bleeding like a wound.

I pointed to it.

"Let's fix this."

So we did.

For the next hour I explained decimals the same way I
explained pistons.

"If you rush it, it misfires."

He laughed — a little.

Then again — louder this time — when he finally solved one on his own.

"You see?" I said.

He nodded, eyes brighter.

"I just needed steps."

"Everybody needs steps," I told him.
"Even grown men."

He didn't know I was talking about myself too.

A week later, a miracle happened.

He walked into the shop with a paper in his hand — held tight, almost scared of losing it.

He didn't speak.

Just handed it to me like it was something sacred.

It was a quiz.

Stamped in purple ink:

84% — ¡MUY BIEN!

I looked at him.

He looked at the floor.

His lips wouldn't stop shaking.

"You earned this," I said quietly.

He nodded.

But then he said:

"My dad won't care."

I walked over, took the quiz gently, and taped it to the shop wall right above my desk — the same place I kept pictures of my own kids.

"There," I said.
"Now someone does."

His throat tightened.

His eyes turned red.

But he didn't cry.

Not yet.

He just breathed.

Deep.

Like his lungs were learning something new.

And in that moment I realized…

I wasn't just helping him with school.

I was teaching him something bigger:

That he wasn't allowed to believe lies about himself anymore.

That he could fight without fists.

That he could win without bruises.

That his mind worked just fine…

…once somebody bothered to hand him the right tools.

CHAPTER 10

Respect

Respect is a strange thing.

Some men demand it.
Some men fear it.
Some men pretend they have it.

But real respect — the kind that sticks to your bones —
comes from how you carry yourself when nobody's
watching.

I didn't plan to teach Tomás that lesson so soon.
Life just threw it at him like it always does.

It started on a Thursday.

School had just let out, and Tomás walked into the shop
with a different kind of silence — the heavy kind, the
kind that follows a storm.

His backpack was torn at the top.
His shirt stretched near the collar, like someone grabbed
it.

I didn't even ask.

I just said, "Sit."

He sat on the stool near my workbench.

Tried to fold his hands, but they kept fidgeting.

Finally, he spoke.

"Some guys were talking," he muttered.
"About me."

I nodded.

He was talking carefully, like if he was defusing a bomb.

"What'd they say?"

"They called me… Vargas's janitor."
He swallowed.
"And they said I smell like engines."
His voice dropped.
"And they said I only got a good grade because you
probably did my homework."

I tightened a bolt a little harder than necessary.

"Did you hit them?" I asked calmly.

His eyes widened.
"No."

"Did you want to?"

His ears turned red.
"…Yes."

"Why didn't you?"

He shrugged.
"They were bigger."

I put the wrench down.

"Tomás.
Look at me."

He did.

"Respect doesn't come from winning fights.
It comes from winning **yourself**."

He blinked slowly.

Didn't understand yet.

So I kept going.

"You don't fight boys who only know how to bark.
Let them talk.
You keep building."

He looked unsure.

Like he wanted to believe me but had lived too long in a
world where talking back meant danger.

Then he asked:

"What if they don't stop?"

"Then you show them something."

"Like what?"

I wiped my hands on a rag.

"Not fists."

He frowned.
"Then what?"

"Your back."

He looked confused.

"When you walk past them," I said, "they need to see a man — not a boy waiting for permission to exist."

He swallowed.

"That's…hard."

"Being a man is hard.
Being a good man is harder."

He nodded slowly.

"We're going to train something new today," I said.

He perked up a little.

"Boxing?"

"No."

I stood tall.

"Posture."

He stared.

"Posture?"

"Sí, mijo. Posture. Shoulders up. Chin level. Eyes forward. Like you're walking into a church or a fight — same stance."

I showed him.

He copied.

Too stiff.

"Relax," I said.

He exhaled.

"Again."

We spent the next twenty minutes walking from one end of the shop to the other.

Back and forth.
Back and forth.

To anyone watching, it probably looked stupid.

But it wasn't.

It was a boy learning how to stop shrinking.

"How do you feel?" I asked after the tenth lap.

"Taller," he said.

"Good. Now talk."

He blinked.
"Talk?"

"Say: 'I'm not here by accident.'"

He hesitated.

Then whispered, "I'm not here by accident."

"Louder."

"I'm not here by accident."

"Again."

"I'm not here by accident!"

Now it sounded like he meant it.

The next day, he came into the shop with a calmness I hadn't seen before.

Not cocky.

Just steady.

"How was school?" I asked.

He shrugged.

"They talked again," he said.
"But I walked past them."

"And?"

"They got quiet."

I smiled.

"And how did you feel?"

He thought for a second.

Then said something so simple, so honest, that it stopped me:

"I felt… like they couldn't reach me anymore."

I nodded.

"That's respect, mijo.
Not from them — from you."

Something changed in him that day.

Not his strength.
Not his height.
Not even his voice.

His belief.

Respect isn't something you demand.

It's something you grow into.

And Tomás was finally — finally — standing at full
height.

CHAPTER 11

The Test

Respect will keep most boys in line.
But *not all of them.*

Some boys don't understand posture.
Some don't understand silence.
Some only understand consequence.

Tomás wasn't trying to prove anything.

Not that day.

He woke up with confidence in his chest — small, but real — like a new muscle he hadn't used before. He walked to school standing how I taught him, shoulders back, eyes forward, not a single flinch in his step.

And for most of the day, it worked.

Whispers stayed whispers.
Stares didn't bother him.
He had a quiz that he passed.
A teacher who finally smiled at him.

He felt...
capable.

Then *Luis Ortega* decided to test him.

Luis was taller.
Meaner.
One of those boys who got loud when teachers weren't
looking.

The kind who confused fear with leadership.

It happened after last bell.

Tomás was walking toward the gate when he heard it.

"Hey, janitor boy!"

He didn't stop.

Didn't turn.

Didn't shrink.

Just kept walking.

I would've been proud.

But boys like Luis hate being ignored.

"Hey!" Luis shouted, footsteps quickening. "I'm talking
to you."

Tomás remembered my rule:

You don't fight boys who only know how to bark.

So he kept going.

Until the hand grabbed his backpack.

Hard.

Pulled him back so fast he almost tripped.

"Where you going, huh?"
Luis sneered in his face.
"You think you're tough now? Just 'cause you work for some mechanic?"

Tomás breathed through his nose — steady like Coach Manny taught him.

"I'm not trying to fight," he said quietly.

Luis smirked.

"That's good. 'Cause you'd lose."

He shoved him.

Not hard.

Just enough to test.

Tomás stepped back.

Controlled.

Calm.

"I don't want trouble," he repeated.

Luis stepped forward, blocking the walkway.

Two other boys moved behind Tomás.

A corner.

A trap.

The kind boys create when they smell change in someone they used to own.

Tomás's heart pounded, but his mind stayed straight.

Like I told him:

Fear doesn't mean weakness.
Fear means you're paying attention.

Luis shoved him again.

Harder this time.

"Come on, Vargas-boy. Show me your posture now."

Tomás closed his eyes for half a second.

He remembered the shop.
The gym.
The mirror.
The stance.

And he remembered the rule:

**You don't hit first...
but you finish what you start.**

When he opened his eyes, something shifted.

He wasn't scared anymore.

He was ready.

Luis swung first.

A wide, sloppy punch made by a boy who thought anger was a weapon.

Tomás stepped back — clean — just like Manny drilled into his feet.

The punch missed by a mile.

Another swing came.
Tomás blocked it.
Not with panic.
With technique.

Luis stumbled forward, off balance.

Tomás didn't counter yet.

He gave him one more chance to walk away.

Luis didn't take it.

He reached for Tomás's shirt.

Tomás reacted — quick, sharp, precise.

One step forward.
One twist of the hips.
A clean jab to the chest — not the face — just enough to
stop his movement.

Luis fell backward onto the concrete, gasping like
someone had deflated him.

The other boys froze.

Tomás didn't raise his fists again.

Didn't puff his chest.
Didn't yell.
Didn't celebrate.

He just breathed.

Steady.

Calm.

Then he walked away.

Not fast.

Not scared.

Just… done.

The next day the principal called him in.

Tomás sat down, expecting the worst.

His father never defended him.
Teachers rarely believed him.
Life usually swung its belt before asking questions.

But the principal — Mrs. Aranda — folded her hands
and sighed.

"I saw the footage," she said.

Tomás swallowed.

"You didn't start that fight."

He nodded once.

"You didn't escalate it."

Another nod.

"And you stopped the moment he hit the ground."

Tomás looked up.

Her face softened.

"This is self-defense, Tomás.
A clean case.
You handled yourself better than most grown men."

He blinked, unsure.

"You're not suspended," she continued.
"But we are calling your father."

His stomach dropped.

"That said…" she added, lowering her voice,
"I want you to know something."

He waited.

"You showed respect — for yourself, for him, for this
school. I'm proud of you."

Tomás's throat tightened.

Nobody had ever said that to him after a fight.

Maybe ever.

He walked out of that office taller than he'd walked in.

Respect wasn't a slogan anymore.

It was a shield.

A stance.

A truth.

And for the first time in his life…

He believed he deserved to stand.

CHAPTER 12

Faith

Faith wasn't something I ever forced on Tomás.

Some people shove religion into kids like it's medicine
—
lávate la boca, say your prayers, behave.

But faith doesn't grow in pressure.

It grows in quiet.

It grows in the spaces between fear and hope.

And Tomás…
he still had a lot of empty spaces inside him.

One Sunday morning, months after the fight, I was getting ready to go to church and he showed up at my shop.

He didn't knock.

Just stood by the open bay door, hands in his pockets, eyes low.

"Why aren't you home?" I asked.

He shrugged.

"Just walking."

"In your school uniform?"

He looked down, confused.

"No… this is my nice shirt."

It wasn't nice.

But he believed it was.

And that made it nice.

"You hungry?" I asked.

He nodded.

I gave him a concha and half my coffee — the kind so strong it wakes sins.

He took one sip and made a face.

"Eso," I laughed. "That's how you know it's good."

He grinned.

Then, out of nowhere, he said:

"Can I… go with you?"

I didn't have to ask where.

I already knew.

We walked to Guardian Angel — the historic, neighborhood church that anchored my community for generations. If you blink, you would miss the red-brick façade that gave it a classic, sturdy presence. Walking towards it, however, it was hard not to notice it's tall bell tower and the steeple so high in the air, the cross above it seemed to touch heaven.

The moment we stepped inside, he stiffened.

Like the air was heavier than outside.

People looked.
Not rudely.
Just surprised.
A boy they didn't recognize.
A man they did.

I placed a hand on his back as I dipped my finger tip in holy water.

"Just breathe," I whispered.

He did.

Slowly.

We sat in the middle pew.

He didn't kneel at first.

Just watched everyone.

The candles.
The stained glass.
The old women with rosaries wrapped around their
fingers like armor.
The kids fidgeting in their little shoes.

Faith is louder on Sundays.

Even the silence has a heartbeat.

Halfway through the service, I walked up to light a
candle.

Not for show.

For my Nino, Roberto.

For the promise I made.
For the boy beside me.
For all the things men don't say out loud.

When I came back, Tomás leaned toward me and
whispered:

"Why do you do that?"

"Do what?"

"Light a candle."

"It's a conversation," I said.

"With God?"

"With myself," I shrugged. "And maybe with God too.
Depends on the day."

He turned that idea over in his head like a tool he'd never
seen before.

"What do you say?" he asked.

"That I'm grateful," I said.
"And that I'm trying."

He nodded like he understood… mostly.

At Communion, when half the church lined up, he stayed
seated, looking unsure.

"You don't have to go," I told him.
"You only go when your heart knows why you're
going."

He relaxed.

Not embarrassed.

Just relieved.

After Mass, when everyone was spilling out into the
sunlight, he lingered by the candles.

One flickered near his hand.

He pointed.

"Is that for somebody?"

"It's for everyone," I said.
"Even people who think they don't deserve one."

He swallowed hard.

"Do I deserve one?"

I looked him dead in the eyes.

"Sí, mijo.
More than you know."

He didn't say anything.

But his breathing changed.

And I could tell something inside him shifted —
not a conversion, not a revelation…
just a quiet opening.

A door no one had ever let him touch before.

On the walk back, he asked softly:

"Do you think God… listens?"

"Yes."

"To everyone?"

"Yes."

"Even to…"
He hesitated.
"…even to people like me?"

I stopped walking.

Turned to him.

"Especially to people like you."

He stared at the ground.

Then whispered something I almost didn't hear:

"I think… I want to talk to Him."

I placed my hand on his shoulder — gently, the way my nino did with me.

"You already are."

That evening, after he left, I sat in the back of the shop
with my old milk crate, thinking.

I'd taught Tomás mechanics.
Respect.
Discipline.
Strength.

But this — this tiny spark of faith?

This wasn't my doing.

This was something bigger.

Some boys grow because you push them.

Others grow because the world forces them.

But some boys grow the moment they realize…

they're worth saving.

CHAPTER 13

The First Job

By the time summer rolled around, Tomás wasn't the same kid who walked into my shop with his shoulders touching his ears.

He walked straighter.
Talked clearer.
Looked people in the eyes — not long, but long enough to be counted.

He still doubted himself sometimes — the world shapes boys like that — but the doubts were quieter now. Easier to push aside.

Which meant he was ready.

Ready for something real.

One Thursday morning, I tossed him a clean rag and said:

"Today, you're taking your first job."

He caught the rag but froze.

"Like… by myself?"

"Not by yourself," I said.
"With me watching."

He nodded, trying to hide the panic.

A white Honda Civic rolled into the bay.
Middle-aged woman.
Kind smile.
She'd been my customer for ten years.

"Morning, Emilio," she said.

"Morning, Mrs. Ruiz. This here is Tomás — mi aprendiz.
He'll be taking care of you today."

Tomás's head snapped toward me like I had betrayed
him.

Mrs. Ruiz smiled warmly.

"Oh! Qué profesional. Nice to meet you, mijo."

Tomás swallowed.

"Nice to meet you, ma'am."

His voice cracked a little, but he didn't hide it.
That was new.

I handed him the work order.

"Oil change. Check fluids. Tire pressure. Air filter."

He read it twice, making sure he didn't miss anything.

Then he got to work.

Slow.
Careful.
Focused.

His hands shook when he removed the oil cap, but he took a breath — steady, like Manny taught him — and continued.

Mrs. Ruiz watched him the whole time, smiling.

"You're doing great," she said.

Tomás didn't look up, but the tips of his ears turned red.

He checked the dipstick twice, even though once was enough.

He lifted the car on the jack without asking me to confirm the height.

He identified a worn air filter on his own and asked Mrs. Ruiz if she wanted a replacement.

Her eyebrows lifted.

"You check everything, huh?"

He nodded.
"Yes, ma'am. We want you safe."

We.

He said *we.*

Not *Emilio.*
Not *the shop.*
We.

That's when I felt something in my chest — a warmth, an ache, pride, and fear all in one.

The kind you get when you realize a boy is starting to believe he belongs somewhere.

When the job was done, Mrs. Ruiz paid and said:

"You take care of him, Emilio."

I smiled.

"He takes care of himself."

Before she left, she slipped Tomás a five-dollar bill.

"For doing it right the first time," she said.

He tried to hand it back.

She shook her head.

"No, mijo. You earned it."

After she drove away, he stood there staring at the bill like it was a medal.

"You can keep it," I told him.

"Really?"

"Really. But I want you to understand something."

He straightened.

"You're not being paid for the oil change."
I tapped his chest.
"You're being paid for your name."

He frowned.
"My name?"

"Sí. When someone pays you, they're trusting you. They're saying your name is worth something."

He looked at the bill again.

Worth something.

That idea landed in him slow and heavy and beautiful.

Later that afternoon he walked around the shop differently.

Not like he owned the place.

Like he respected it.

He tightened bolts without me asking.
Sorted tools without being told.
Checked a tire just because it looked low.

He wasn't playing mechanic anymore.

He was becoming one.

And when he swept the floor at closing time, he didn't sweep like a boy doing chores.

He swept like a man taking pride in the ground beneath his feet.

Right before he left, he said:

"Emilio?"

"Yes, mijo."

"Do you think… do you think I can do this? For real?"

I looked him in the eyes.

Not like a boss.

Not like a teacher.

Like a man talking to another man who just needed
someone to believe in him.

"Tomás…
I wouldn't be teaching you if you couldn't."

His chin trembled — just once — before he steadied it.

"Thank you," he whispered.

"You don't thank me," I said.
"You show me."

He nodded.

Then he walked out of the shop with the same five
dollars still in his fist — not to spend, but to remember.

Because a boy never forgets the first time the world told
him he was good at something.

CHAPTER 14

The Fighter

Coach Manny had a rule:

"No kid touches the ring until they've learned to lose."

Most boys don't like that rule.
They want the gloves.
They want the punches.
They want to feel tough before they learn how to be patient.

But Tomás wasn't most boys.

He didn't want to fight.
Didn't want to show off.
Didn't want to knock anyone down.

He just wanted to stop feeling small.

Which, in Manny's world, made him exactly the kind of kid worth training.

One Friday evening, months after Tomás had been doing drills, bag work, shadowboxing, and footwork until his legs shook, Manny called us over.

"You ready?" he asked Tomás.

Tomás looked confused.

"For what?"

Manny pointed to the ring.

"Three rounds. Light sparring."

Tomás froze.

"Coach… no. I'm not—"

"You are," Manny said.
"But you don't see it yet."

He handed Tomás gloves.

Red ones.

Not loaners.

My heart caught.

Real gloves belong to real fighters.

Tomás slid them on with shaking hands.

"You don't have to win," I told him quietly.
"You just have to show up."

He nodded, swallowed hard, and climbed into the ring.

On the other side stood **Marco**, a fifteen-year-old with faster hands and a little too much confidence. Not a bully — just a kid who'd been told he was talented and believed it.

Manny looked at them both.

"No headshots. Light contact. You listen to my voice or I stop it."

Marco touched gloves casually.

Tomás touched back like he was holding something fragile.

Then the bell rang.

First round was messy.

Tomás backpedaled too much.
Forgot to breathe.
Kept lifting his chin — the worst habit.

Marco tapped him twice in the ribs, nothing heavy, just reminders.

Tap.
Tap.

Tomás's eyes filled with panic.
His feet tangled.
He tripped over himself more than the punches.

But he didn't quit.

That alone said something.

When the bell rang, he stumbled back to the corner,
breathing loud.

"I can't," he whispered.

"You can," Manny said, wiping sweat from his face.
"You're not here to be perfect. You're here to learn."

I leaned on the ropes.

"You already survived one round," I told him.
"Everyone survives the first one. Only fighters come
back for the second."

He inhaled.
Exhaled.
Nodded.

Second round.

Something changed.

Not in Marco — he stayed sharp, cocky, controlled.

But in Tomás.

He remembered his feet.

Forward.
Back.
Side.
Side.

He remembered his hands.

Up.
Tight.
Protect your space.

Marco swung wide.
Tomás ducked — clean.
So clean the crowd murmured.

Even Marco blinked like he hadn't expected it.

Tomás didn't punch back.
Not yet.

He didn't need to.

He just needed to be *in* it.

Midway through the round, Marco threw a short hook.

Tomás blocked it — textbook perfect — and pivoted
away like Manny drilled into him ten thousand times.

The bagwork suddenly meant something.

The drills meant something.

The mirror meant something.

The fear meant something.

He wasn't fighting Marco.

He was fighting every lie he'd been fed.

You're dumb.
You're weak.
You're a nobody.

Every swing was a chance to prove those voices wrong.

The bell rang.

Tomás stood taller going back to the corner.

Not proud.
Not cocky.

Just… present.

A man who knew he belonged in the space he was
standing.

Third round.

Manny leaned over him.

"Okay, mijo. Listen. Marco's faster. He might be stronger. But he's not smarter. Let him miss. Make him work. And if you see an opening, you take it — clean *pero con huevos*."

Tomás nodded.

The bell rang.

Marco came in aggressive.

Too aggressive.

He thought he needed to dominate the last round.

Tomás didn't panic.

He stepped back.
Not running — respecting space.

Marco lunged.

That's when it happened.

One moment — wild energy.
Next moment — clarity.

Marco left his right side open.

For half a second.

Maybe less.

Tomás didn't think.

He reacted.

A sharp, perfect jab.

Right to the chin.

Not reckless.
Not angry.

Controlled.

Disciplined.

Clean.

With the force of a Hemi V8!

Marco staggered.

The crowd reacted.

Manny's eyebrows shot up.

I felt my chest get tight, the good kind of tight — pride
wrapped around fear wrapped around love.

The bell rang.

Match over.

Marco pulled his mouthguard out and grinned.

"Nice shot, bro," he said as he gave him a fist bump.

Just like that.

Respect earned the real way.

Not through fear.

Through presence.

When Tomás climbed out of the ring, his legs were
shaking.
Sweat ran down his face.
Hair plastered to his forehead.

But his eyes?

His eyes were new.

He looked at me and said:

"I felt… strong."

Not violent.
Not superior.

Just strong.

I put my hand on his shoulder — the way Roberto used
to do with me.

"You are," I said.

And that night, as we walked out of the gym into the
warm desert air, he carried himself like a boy who finally
understood something important:

You don't fight to hurt.
You fight to stand.

And he was finally standing.

CHAPTER 15

The Man

The summer before his freshman year of high school,
Tomás finally started looking like he belonged in his own
skin.

Not because he grew taller…
though he did.

Not because his shoulders widened…
though they did.

Not because he could throw a cleaner jab or fix a timing
belt without breaking a sweat…

But because something inside him had settled.

Boys who grow up scared move like the world is always
about to drop something on them.
Boys who grow up believed-in move differently.

And Tomás was finally moving like someone who
believed in himself — at least a little.

One day after work, I found him in the back of the shop
rebuilding a carburetor I hadn't even assigned him.

He had taken it apart piece by piece, cleaned every part, polished every screw, laying them out on a rag like a surgeon prepping instruments.

"You're working late," I said.

He didn't look up.

"I wanted to practice," he said.
"This one's older. Harder."

I smiled.

"The hard stuff is where men are made."

He tightened one last screw, wiped his forehead, and leaned back.

"Emilio… can I ask you something?"

"Claro."

He hesitated, twisting the rag in his hands.

"What… what am I supposed to do when I get older?"

I pulled up a crate.

"What do you mean?"

"I mean… what am I going to be? Am I supposed to be a mechanic like you? Or go to college? Or… something else? I don't want to disappoint anybody."

I exhaled slowly.

There it was.

The question every boy asks the moment he realizes he is no longer one.

"What do *you* want?" I asked.

He blinked.

"I… don't know."

"That's okay."

He frowned.

"No it's not. Everyone else knows. All the kids at school already talk about college or the military or jobs. I'm just… here."

I tapped the carburetor between us.

"You're not 'just' anywhere. You're learning. You're building."

He looked unconvinced.

So I tried something different.

"When I was your age," I said, "I thought I would run a giant shop, with twenty mechanics working under me. I thought I'd be a padrino by twenty-five, rich by thirty, retired by forty."

"And… that didn't happen?"

I laughed.

"No, mijo. Life doesn't follow blueprints. It follows character."

He tilted his head.

"What does that mean?"

"It means who you are decides where you go — not the other way around."

He took that in.
Slowly.
Carefully.

"So… who am I?"

I leaned forward.

"You're someone who doesn't quit. You're someone who listens. Someone who fights only when he has to. Someone who fixes things. Someone who respects people — even when they don't deserve it."

He swallowed hard.

"Is that… good?"

"It's rare," I said.
"And rare is valuable."

He looked down, blinking fast.

"Do you think I could go to trade school? Or maybe college? Or maybe something with engines… or construction… or—"

"You could do all of that," I said.
"You've got options now."

He looked at his hands — stained with grease, knuckles still bruised from sparring.

"These hands…" he whispered. "Sometimes I think they're only good for breaking things."

I shook my head.

"No, Tomás.
These hands build."

Then he asked something so honest it stopped the air between us:

"Do you think I'll ever be… a good man?"

I felt my throat tighten.

Because that wasn't a question about the future.
It was a question about his past — his father's words, his bruised confidence, every lie he ever swallowed.

I put my hand on his shoulder.

"You already are," I said.
"You just haven't grown into the full size of it yet."

He breathed in deep — the kind of breath you take when someone finally hands you permission to hope.

By the end of that summer, he wasn't just helping in the shop.

He was running things.

He greeted customers.
Took small jobs.
Handled tools with confidence.
Explained repairs clearly.
Even taught one of the younger kids how to air up tires properly.

And one day, I caught him doing something that nearly knocked me over with pride:

He taped one of *his own* assignments — a history essay with a 92% — right next to the oil-change chart on the wall.

Not hiding it.
Displaying it.

Claiming it.

Like a man who finally believed his name meant
something.

That night, while closing the shop, he looked around and
said:

"This place feels like home."

I nodded.

"It is, mijo."

And that's when it hit me:

He wasn't asking me who he was anymore.
He was starting to answer the question himself.

Not a boy.
Not a scared kid.
Not a nobody.

But a young man —
one with a future,
one with a voice,
one with a path forming under his feet.

He just didn't know how far that path would take him.

Not yet.

But soon.

Very soon.

CHAPTER 16

The First Cracks with His Father

Tomás had grown in ways his father never expected —
ways he *didn't* understand,
ways he *didn't* control.

And men like Ray Salazar don't handle that well.

Pride in a father is supposed to sound like:

Look at my boy.
He's becoming something.
He's better than I ever was.

But Ray was built different.

His pride was warped, dented over years of bad luck, bad
choices, and bad company.
Sometimes a man who never learned to lift anything will
try to lift his son —
only to crush him instead.

The first crack happened on a Wednesday.

Tomás walked into the shop later than usual — not late, but not early either. His shoulders were tense, his jaw tight, his eyes darker than I'd ever seen them.

He grabbed a broom and started sweeping without saying a word.

After a few minutes, I walked over.

"What happened?"

He didn't look up.

"Nothing."

"Try again."

He swallowed, hands tightening around the broom handle.

"My dad saw my history essay."

"Ah."
I waited.
"That's good, isn't it?"

"No."

I leaned against the toolbox.

"What'd he say?"

Tomás finally stopped sweeping.
He stared at the floor.

"He asked me who wrote it for me."

I closed my eyes.

"And when I told him I did it… he laughed."
His voice cracked.
"He said people like us don't get A's. That I should stop
pretending I'm smart."

Slow burn.
Hot rage.
I felt it like oil about to catch fire.

But I kept my voice calm.

"Come here," I said.

He walked over slowly, broom dragging behind him.

"Look at me."

He did.

And I swear, for a moment, I didn't see the young man
he was becoming.

I saw the little boy he used to be — the one who learned
to shrink so other people didn't feel small.

"That man," I said carefully, "is wrong."

Tomás blinked fast, trying not to show emotion.

"He's my dad," he whispered.

"I know," I said.
"And he's still wrong."

He wiped his nose on his sleeve.

"What if he's right? What if I just got lucky? What if—"

"No," I interrupted sharply.
"Listen to me. There is nothing about you that is luck.
Not your grades. Not your discipline. Not your strength.
You built this."

"But he doesn't see it."

I nodded.

"Some people don't see what scares them."

He frowned.

"Why would I scare him?"

"Because you're becoming a man," I said.
"And he knows he had nothing to do with it."

That landed.

Hard.

He leaned against the counter, breathing like he'd just finished sparring.

I didn't push him.

I knew he'd open-up slowly.

Two days later, Ray came to the shop.

He didn't smile.
Didn't say hello.
Just barged in like he always did, chest out, voice loud.

"Tomás! Vámonos ya. We're leaving."

Tomás stiffened.

"I'm working, Dad."

"Working?" Ray scoffed.
"You're a kid. You don't work. Let's go."

I stepped forward.

"He's finishing a job."

Ray's eyes narrowed.

"Since when do you tell my son what to do?"

"Since you brought him to me," I said.
"And agreed to let me train him."

Ray scoffed again.

"Train him? Train him for what? To be a grease monkey like you?"

I didn't flinch.

But Tomás did.

He stepped between us — not aggressively, not scared — just present.

"Dad," he said quietly, "don't talk to him like that."

Ray blinked.

Confusion.
Surprise.
Offense.

"You talking back to me?"

Tomás swallowed.

"No. I'm asking you to stop."

Ray's voice dropped into danger.

"You think you're a man now?"

Tomás didn't answer.

Didn't shrink.

Didn't bow.

Just stood there, steady.

Ray stepped closer — too close.

"You're nothing without me," he hissed.
"Nothing."

Tomás's jaw flexed.

And with a calm he shouldn't have had at his age, he said:

"That's not true anymore."

Silence.

A heavy one.
A breaking one.

Ray stared, breathing hard, chest heaving.

Then he turned on his heel and left the shop without another word.

The bell above the door rattled behind him, shaking like it understood something had just fractured for good.

Tomás stood still long after his father left.

Didn't speak.
Didn't move.

Just breathed.

Finally, he whispered:

"I didn't mean to disrespect him."

"You didn't," I said.

"He's still my dad."

"Yes."

"So why does it hurt?"

"Because you're finally growing," I said.
"And growth always hurts the one who refuses to grow
with you."

He looked down at his hands — big, capable, strong.

Hands that used to shake.

Hands that used to bruise.

Hands that now rebuilt engines and defended himself and
wrote essays and made choices.

"He hates me," Tomás said quietly.

"No," I said.
"He fears losing control of you. And that's not the same thing."

He swallowed.

"Does it get better?"

"Yes," I said.
"When you build a life stronger than the one you came from."

He looked around the shop — the place that held all his beginnings.

"It kind of feels like I already am."

And that…

That was the first time he allowed himself to believe that maybe, just maybe—

He wasn't his father's son anymore.

He was becoming his own man.

CHAPTER 17

Preparing for the Baptism

Tomás didn't say it out loud at first.

He just **started showing up differently**.

Quieter, but not sad.
Focused, but not tense.
Like something inside him was shifting into place — a puzzle piece he didn't know he'd been missing.

It began the week after the blow-up with his father.

He walked into the shop carrying a small white envelope. He kept it in his pocket, touching it every few minutes, like he was checking if it was still real.

I didn't ask.

Some things need to unfold on their own.

That Sunday, he met me outside Guardian Angel Church.

Not planned.

Not coincidence.

He just… showed up.

His hair was combed.
Shirt tucked in.
Shoes dusty but trying.

"Morning," he said quietly.

"Morning, mijo."

We walked inside together.

He didn't sit by the aisle like usual.
He sat closer to the front — still two rows back, but
closer to the altar, closer to the candles, closer to
whatever answer he was searching for.

During the service he watched everything:

The priest's hands.
The people praying.
The choir's voices.
The babies being held.
The men bowing their heads.

He looked like someone trying to understand the shape of
something invisible.

After Mass, he waited until the last person left before
approaching the little baptismal font.

He ran his fingers along the stone edge.

"What's this water for?" he asked.

"For beginnings," I said.

He nodded slowly.

"I think I want one."

That week, he came straight to the shop after school and pulled me aside.

"I talked to Father Miguel," he said.

"Oh yeah?"

He nodded.

"I asked him what someone needs if… if they want to get baptized at my age."

I didn't react big.

Didn't crowd him.

Just listened.

"What did he say?"

"That I need a sponsor. Someone who walks with me. Someone who guides me. Someone I trust."

His voice shook a little on that last part.

He added:

"He said… a padrino."

I swallowed.

My hands started sweating inside my gloves — the mechanic's kind of nerves, the ones you only get when something important is about to fall into place.

But Tomás didn't ask anything yet.

He just stood there, fidgeting with that white envelope like he was afraid it might burn through his pocket.

I nodded.

"That's true. A padrino isn't just a title. It's a promise. A big one."

"A big one," he echoed.

He stared at the floor.

"Do you think… do you think I'm ready?"

I stepped closer.

"You've been ready since the day you walked into this shop," I said.
"You just didn't know it."

His throat tightened.
He looked away.

Then he whispered:

"Father Miguel says baptism is like… starting new."

"It is," I said.

"But what if my dad doesn't support it?"

I placed a steady hand on his shoulder.

"Not all beginnings are approved by the people we started with."

He nodded.

It hurt him.
But he understood.

He was beginning to choose his own life.

A few days later, at the shop, he took out the white envelope and handed it to me.

"What's this?" I asked.

"My forms," he said.
"For the baptism."

I opened it.

The papers were neat, filled out carefully, every letter placed like it mattered — because it did.

Under "Age," he had written **15**.

Under "Reason for Baptism," he had written:

I want to walk the right way.

I looked at him, but he kept his eyes down.

"Tomás," I said.
"This is beautiful."

He shrugged.

"Father Miguel says I should pick a saint too… I've been reading about them. Some of their stories are crazy."

"Good crazy," I said.

"Not all of them," he smirked.

Fair point.

Then his face grew serious again.

"Emilio… is it weird to get baptized this late?"

"No," I said.
"It's beautiful. It means you're choosing it."

He breathed in slowly.

"I want to prepare right. I don't want to mess it up."

"You won't," I said.
"But preparation doesn't start with clothes or candles."

He frowned.

"Then what?"

"It starts here," I said, tapping my chest.
"And here," tapping my temple.

He nodded.

Then:

"Will you… help me?"

"Always."

Over the next few weeks, Tomás began changing again.

Not like before — this was deeper.
Not louder — this was quieter.

He spoke gently.
Listened more.
Worked with more intention.
Went to church on his own.

Stopped responding to insults at school.
Stopped trying to please people who didn't see him.

He wasn't becoming a different person.

He was becoming who he was meant to be.

One night, after closing the shop, he lingered by the doorway.

Hands in his pockets.
Breathing heavy like a man about to lift something emotional.

"There's something I need to ask you," he said.

His voice cracked.

But he continued:

"And I… I want to do it right."

I felt something pull tight in my chest.

Because I suddenly knew—

The question was coming.

The one he'd been carrying.
The one I'd been waiting for my whole life.

He looked at me with eyes full of fear and hope tangled together.

"Emilio…"

He swallowed.

"I… I want to ask you something important."

But he didn't finish.

Not yet.

Some questions take courage.
Some moments take timing.

This one needed both.

And both were finally coming to him…

Just not all at once.

CHAPTER 18

The Ask

Some moments announce themselves.

This one didn't.

It came in quietly — like most important things do — wrapped in an ordinary afternoon with the shop door half open and the smell of oil and dust hanging in the air.

Tomás stayed late that day.

Not working.
Not cleaning.

Just… there.

He leaned against the workbench, rolling a bolt between his fingers, dropping it, picking it up again. His shoulders rose and fell too fast for a kid who knew how to breathe through pressure.

I finished locking up the toolbox and waited.

Men don't rush moments like this.

Finally, he spoke.

"Emilio… can we talk?"

I nodded and sat down on the milk crate.

"Claro, mijo."

He stood there a second longer, like his feet didn't trust the floor.

Then he sat across from me.

"I talked to Father Miguel again."

I didn't interrupt.

"He says my baptism can be next month," he continued. "He says I'm ready."

I smiled.

"You are."

He nodded, but didn't smile back.

His hands shook a little now.

"There's just one thing left."

I felt my chest tighten — not fear, not hope — something older. Something buried.

"The padrino," he said.

There it was.

The word that had followed me my whole life without
ever landing.

He swallowed hard.

"He told me I need to choose someone who—"
His voice cracked.
"—who walks with me. Who teaches me how to live
right. Who doesn't disappear when things get hard."

I stared at the concrete floor.

The stains.
The cracks.
The years.

"I've been thinking about it a lot," he went on.
"About who's always been there. Who showed me how
to work. How to stand. How to fight without becoming
angry. How to believe in myself when I couldn't."

My throat burned.

I still didn't look up.

Because some dreams feel dangerous to meet head-on.

He shifted closer.

"I don't have much family I can trust," he said quietly.
"And I know… I know I'm not blood."

I closed my eyes.

Here it comes, Roberto, I thought.
If you're still listening… help me breathe.

Then he said it.

Not loud.
Not dramatic.

Just honest.

"Emilio… would you be my nino?"

The shop went silent.

No radios.
No engines.
No city noise.

Just the sound of a promise finally being offered back.

I felt my hands tremble — the same hands that had fixed engines, lifted children, buried parents, and carried a dream I thought had expired.

I looked at him.

Really looked.

Not the boy who walked in scared and shrinking.
Not the kid everyone called a nobody.

But a young man who chose his own life.

"Tomás," I said, my voice rough, "you don't ask that lightly."

"I know," he said.
"I've thought about it every day."

I stood up slowly.

I didn't want to scare the moment.

"I waited my whole life for that question," I admitted.

His eyes widened.

"You did?"

I nodded.

"When my nino died, I promised myself I'd be that man for someone one day. And for a long time, I thought… maybe God forgot."

My voice cracked.

"Maybe He didn't," Tomás whispered.

I laughed softly through wet eyes.

"Maybe He didn't."

I stepped closer and placed my hand on his shoulder —
firm, steady, like Roberto used to do with me.

"Sí," I said.
"Sí, mijo. I would be honored."

His breath hitched.

He nodded hard, like if he stopped moving he might fall
apart.

Then he hugged me.

Not quick.
Not awkward.

The kind of hug that carries years of unsaid thank-yous
and saved tears.

And I held him — not like a boss, not like a teacher —
but like a man who finally understood what he'd been
preparing for all along.

In that moment, I wasn't nobody's nino anymore.

I was **his**.

And he wasn't a nobody.

He never had been.

CHAPTER 19

The Baptism

The morning of the baptism, the church smelled like wax, flowers, and new beginnings.

Tomás stood beside me near the altar, hands folded, shoulders straight, breathing slow. He wore a white shirt that didn't quite fit his arms anymore — he'd grown — and dress shoes that still felt strange on his feet.

But he didn't fidget.

Didn't shrink.

He belonged there.

People filled the pews quietly. A few familiar faces from the shop. Mrs. Ruiz. Coach Manny. Even some teachers from school. Folks who had watched him change without always knowing how.

His father wasn't there.

Tomás had asked me the night before if that was okay.

I told him the truth.

"God shows up even when people don't."

That was enough.

Father Miguel smiled at us as he began.

"Today," he said, "we welcome someone who has chosen faith not because it was handed to him… but because he walked toward it."

I felt Tomás inhale deeply beside me.

When the time came, Father Miguel turned to me.

"And you," he said gently, "as padrino — are you prepared to guide him, support him, and walk with him in faith and in life?"

My chest tightened.

This was it.

Not a dream.
Not a promise.
A calling.

"I am," I said.
My voice steady.
My heart wide open.

Tomás stepped forward.

The water touched his forehead.

Simple.
Sacred.

"I baptize you in the name of the Father, and of the Son, and of the Holy Spirit."

Tomás closed his eyes.

When he opened them again, something in his face had softened — not weaker, not smaller — but lighter.

Like a burden he never named had finally been set down.

I placed my hand on his shoulder.

The same way Roberto once placed his hand on mine.

The circle closed.

Afterward, outside the church, the sun hit just right.

Tomás laughed with people. Took photos. Ate too many cookies. Looked embarrassed when Mrs. Ruiz kissed his cheek and called him *un muchacho bueno*.

Coach Manny clapped him on the back.

"Proud of you, kid."

Tomás smiled — not shy, not unsure.

Just proud.

And for the first time in a long time…

So was I.

CHAPTER 20

Nobody's Nino

Life didn't turn magical after that.

Bills still came.
Cars still broke down.
The shop still smelled like oil and sweat.

But something had shifted.

Tomás kept growing.

Graduated.
Chose trade school.
Kept boxing — not to fight, but to stay sharp.
Worked full-time at the shop.

One day, we put his name on the door:

Vargas Auto & Body
— with Tomás Salazar

He never asked.

He just earned it.

People started calling him *sir*.

Kids started asking him questions.

One afternoon, I caught him teaching a nervous boy how to hold a wrench — patient, steady, kind.

I watched from the back, quiet.

And that's when it hit me.

I didn't raise him to replace me.

I raised him to continue something.

One evening, years later, as we closed the shop, he asked me:

"You ever think about Nino Roberto?"

I smiled.

"Every day."

He nodded.

"I think he'd be proud."

I looked at him — really looked — and felt a peace I never expected to know.

"I think so too."

As the sun dropped behind the buildings, Tomás locked up and said something that made me laugh.

"You know… some people still don't understand how important a nino is."

I shrugged.

"They don't have to."

He smiled.

"Because I do."

And in that moment, I understood something simple and true:

I was never nobody's nino.

I was just waiting for the right one to find me.

THE END

ABOUT THE AUTHOR

JESUS J. TERAN is a Marine Corps Veteran and life-long educator and musician. He has been a principal of several schools in El Paso, Texas. He earned a Master of Education degree from the University of Texas at El Paso.